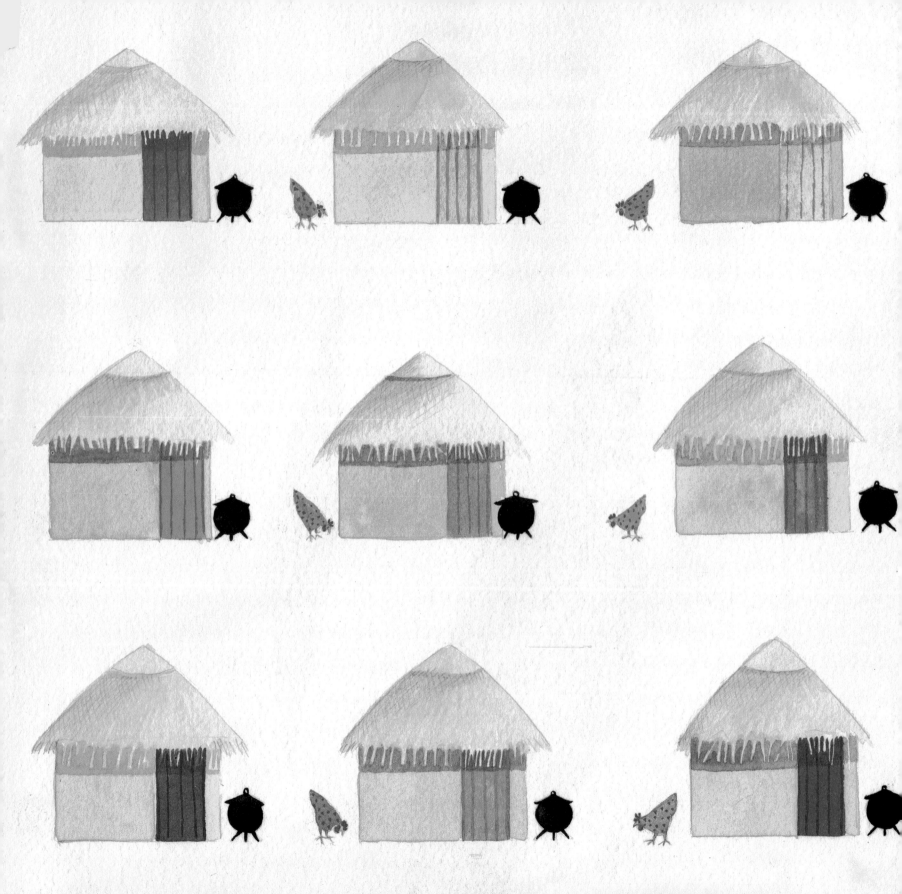

Mama Panya's Pancakes

We'd like to dedicate this book to:
Ben Rerucha and George Pinkham, the authors of our childhood love of stories;
and to the Lisle Wild and Wacky Writers and the Monday SCBWI Group,
for all their love, support and sustenance – M. & R. C.

For my Father and Margaret,
and for Lily, Annabel and George, with love – J. C.

Barefoot Books
124 Walcot Street
Bath BA1 5BG

Text copyright © 2005 by Mary and Rich Chamberlin
Illustrations copyright © 2005 by Julia Cairns
The moral right of Mary and Rich Chamberlin to be identified as the authors
and Julia Cairns to be identified as the illustrator of this work has been asserted

First published in Great Britain in 2005 by Barefoot Books Ltd

This book was typeset in Legacy
The illustrations were prepared in watercolour

Graphic design by Louise Millar
Colour separation by Grafiscan, Verona
Printed and bound in Hong Kong by South China Printing Co. Ltd

This book has been printed on 100% acid-free paper

Hardback ISBN 1-84148-160-2

British Cataloguing-in-Publication Data:
a catalogue record for this book is available from the British Library

1 3 5 7 9 8 6 4 2

Mama Panya's Pancakes

A Village Tale from Kenya

written by

Mary and Rich Chamberlin

illustrated by

Julia Cairns

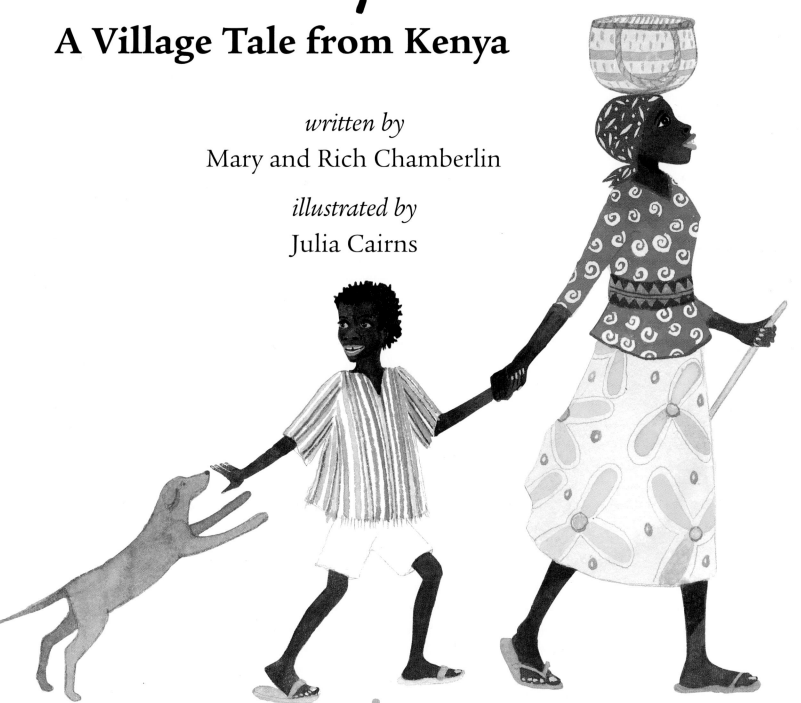

Barefoot Books
Celebrating Art and Story

Mama Panya sang
as she kicked sand
with her bare feet,
dousing the
breakfast fire.
   'Adika, hurry up,'
she called cheerfully.
'Today, we go
to market.'

'Surprise! I'm one step ahead of you, Mama.' Adika stood in the doorway, dressed in his finest shirt and cleanest shorts. 'I'm ready.' Now Mama Panya had to hurry.

After storing her pots, gathering her bag and slipping her feet into her sandals, Mama Panya called, 'I'm ready too, Adika. Where are you?'

'Here I am, Mama — two steps ahead of you.' He sat under the baobab tree, Mama Panya's walking stick in hand.

'Why, yes you are.' She accepted the stick and led them down the road.

'What will you get at the market, Mama?'

'Oh, a little bit and a little bit more.'

'Are you making pancakes today, Mama?'

'You are a smart one. I guess I can't surprise you.'

'Yay! How many pancakes will you make?'

Mama fingered two coins folded in the cloth tied around her waist. 'A little bit and a little bit more.'

Rounding the corner, they saw Mzee Odolo sitting by the river. 'Habari za asubuhi?' Mama asked softly, so she wouldn't chase away the fish.

Adika blurted out, 'We're having pancakes tonight, please come.'

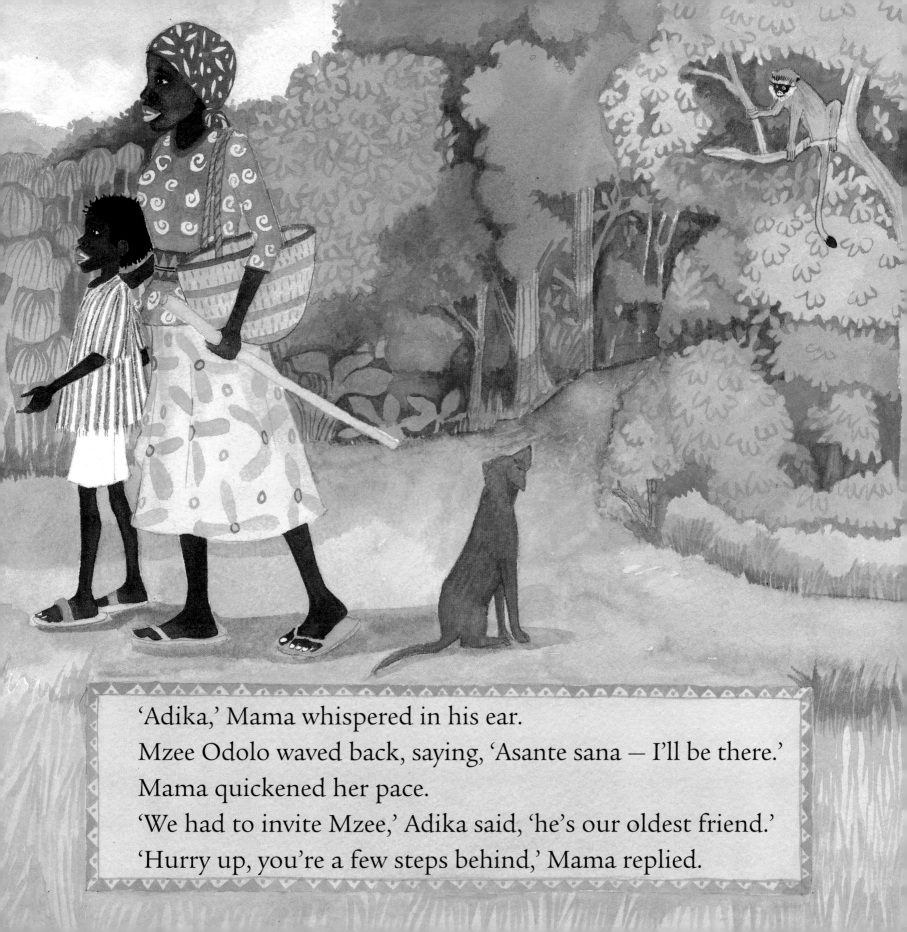

'Adika,' Mama whispered in his ear.

Mzee Odolo waved back, saying, 'Asante sana — I'll be there.'

Mama quickened her pace.

'We had to invite Mzee,' Adika said, 'he's our oldest friend.'

'Hurry up, you're a few steps behind,' Mama replied.

'Look, Mama, it's Sawandi and Naiman.' Adika's friends tapped long reeds against the thighs of their cattle, moving them along. 'I'll be just a few steps ahead.'

'Wait, Adika!' Mama called.

Mama hadn't gone too far before he returned.

'They'd be happy to come,' Adika panted.

Mama Panya frowned, thinking about the coins in her wrap.

'Ohhh! How many people will that be?'

'Let's see. Sawandi, Naiman, you and me,' Adika counted. 'And Mzee Odolo, that's only five.'

'Aiii! How many pancakes do you think I can make today, son?'

'I'm one step ahead of you, Mama. You'll have a little bit and a little bit more. That's enough.'

At the market, there were many buyers and sellers trading fruits, spices and vegetables.

Adika spotted his school friend Gamila at her plantain stand. 'Mama, pancakes are her favourite.'

'Now, now — don't you...' and before she could finish he ran to greet her.

Mama tried to catch up, arriving just in time to hear, 'You will come, won't you?'

'Of course,' Gamila replied.

Mama shot a stare at Adika and quickly grabbed his hand, whisking him away.

'Mama, we'll be able to stretch the flour.'

'Ai-Yi! How much do you think I can stretch flour, son?'

Adika waved his hand in the air. 'Oh, a little bit and a little bit more.'

At the flour stand Mama said, 'Adika, you sit here.'
After greeting Bibi and Bwana Zawenna, Mama asked,
'What can you give me for my money?' She offered the
larger of the two coins to Bibi Zawenna, who scooped a
cup of flour on to a piece of brown paper.

Adika popped up. 'Mama's making pancakes today.
Can you come?'

'Oh, how wonderful! I think we can give a little more for that coin.' Bwana Zawenna put a second cup on to the paper, then tied it up with string. 'We'll see you later.'

Mama tucked the package into her bag. 'Ai-Yi-Yi! You and I will be lucky to share half a pancake.'

'But Mama, we have a little bit and a little bit more.'

'Come Adika, keep up with me. We may have just enough left for a small chilli pepper.'

'Leave it to me Mama, I'll get a good one.'

'No Adika!' she cried out, but he ran ahead to Rafiki Kaya's spice table.

Mama got there just in time to hear, 'Mama's making pancakes tonight, can you come?'

'I'd love to!' Kaya exclaimed. She grabbed the coin from Mama's hand and replaced it with the plumpest pepper. 'That's just enough! Thanks for inviting me.'

Mama just sighed.

They headed home.
'How many people did we invite for pancakes tonight?'

Adika, skipping two steps ahead, sang his reply,
'All of our friends, Mama.'

Mama piled small twigs and sticks into the firepit.

Adika ran to fetch a pail of water.

Mama crushed the chilli pepper in a pot, while Adika added some water. She stirred in all the flour, seeing there would be none to save.

Mama poured a dollop into the oiled pan on the fire.

Sawandi and Naiman were the first to arrive shouting, 'Hodi!' Adika called, 'Karibu' to welcome them. They carried two leather drinking-gourds filled with milk and a small pail of butter. 'Mama Panya, we have extra from our cattle.'

Mzee Odolo came soon after. 'Old man river has given us three fish today.'

Gamila arrived with a plantain bunch perched on her head. 'They go very well with pancakes.'

Bibi and Bwana Zawenna brought a
package filled with more flour and handed
it to Adika. 'Store this away for later.'

When Rafiki Kaya arrived, she brought
handfuls of salt and cardamom spice,
along with her thumb piano.

And the feast began, as they sat under the baobab tree
to eat Mama Panya's pancakes.

Afterwards, Kaya played the thumb piano and Mzee
Odolo sang slightly off key.

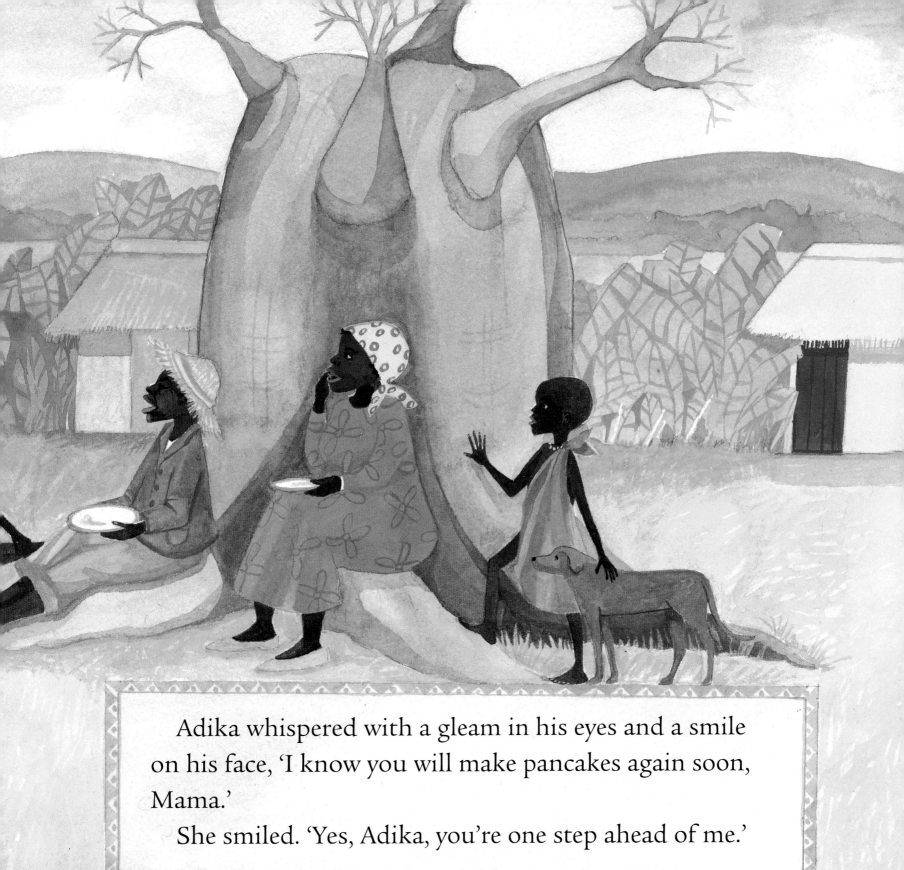

Adika whispered with a gleam in his eyes and a smile on his face, 'I know you will make pancakes again soon, Mama.'

She smiled. 'Yes, Adika, you're one step ahead of me.'

Village Life in Kenya

People

Kenya is made up of many different peoples. Most are Black Africans. There are also Asians, Europeans and others. Many Kenyan people, like Adika and Mama Panya, live in rural areas.

Village Life

Most village people farm and take care of cows, goats and chickens. Others might work on a tea or coffee plantation. When their work is done for the day, villagers tell stories under the stars, and listen to the music of the thumb piano, or 'mbira' (*mm-**beer**-ah*).

School

Children like Adika go to school, but it is often a long walk to their classroom. Very few Kenyan families own cars and there are not many paved roads. Where the government has not been able to open schools, many villages have set up their own classes. These are called Harambee (*hah-**ram**-bay*), which means 'pulling together'. Harambee is also Kenya's national motto.

After School

When they are not at school, older children help with chores such as collecting firewood and taking care of their younger brothers and sisters. They also have time to play — games such as bao, an African board game of strategy, and football are common. Running is also popular.

Walking to Market

On their walk to the market, Adika and Mama Panya see many animals, insects, reptiles and plants. Here are a few examples:

Agama or **Rainbow Lizard** — mjusi (*mm-**joo**-see*)
Male rainbow lizards have pretty red heads and blue bodies. They love to bob up and down, doing push-ups.

Acacia Tree — muwati (*moo-**wah**-tee*)
Also called the thorn tree. Sharp spikes surround the leaves, which are eaten by giraffes.

Baobab Tree — mbuyu (*mm-**boo**-yoo*)
A large tree, often called the Tree of Life, because it stores so much water. Its branches look like exposed roots, but it's not upside down.

Butterfly — kipepeo (*kee-pay-**pay**-oh*)
There are many kinds of butterflies in Kenya. You might see swallowtails, which are the largest butterflies in the world, with a wingspan of up to 23 centimetres.

Goat — mbuzi (*mm-**boo**-zee*)
The Small East African Goat is found all over Kenya. These goats can survive on land that is almost barren, yet still produce lots of milk.

Maasai Cattle — Mmasai ng'ombe (*mm-**mah**-sigh **ngom**-bay*)
Many Kenyan tribes measure their wealth in accordance with the number of cattle they own. Maasai cattle are used mostly for their milk.

Mongoose — nguchiro (*ngoo-**chee**-row*)
These weasel-like creatures live in large families and feed on rodents, birds and even snakes. Although they are cousins of hyenas, they are very friendly and are sometimes kept as pets.

Palm Tree — mivumo (*mee-**voo**-mo*)
There are many species of palms in Kenya. Palm fruit, leaves and bark are used in lots of products, such as soap, roofing materials and rope.

Tilapia — ngege (***ngay**-gay*)
Tilapia can live in harsh conditions, like the hot, salty and alkaline waters of Lake Nakuru.

Speaking Kiswahili

Kenyans speak many languages, but the main ones are Kiswahili and English. Swahili refers to a group of people, also known as the Waswahili, who live along the east coast of Africa, from Somalia to Mozambique. The word 'Swahili' literally means 'coast people' and 'Kiswahili' means 'speaking the language of the coast people'. Kiswahili is a mixture of Bantu, a native African language, and Arabic, a Middle Eastern one.

In a village like Adika's, people might speak three languages: a local language, Kiswahili and English. Greetings are expected upon meeting someone; it is considered rude not to greet another in the appropriate way. As a visitor, you may hear the simple greeting, 'Jambo', which means 'Hello'.

Kiswahili Greetings

Asante sana (*uh-**sahn**-tay **sahn**-ah*) — thank you

Bibi (***bee**-bee*) — lady, madam, miss

Bwana (*buh-**wah**-na*) — sir or mister

Habari za asubuhi? (*ha-**bar**-ee zah ah-suh-**boo**-ee*) — what's new this morning?

Hodi (***hoe**-dee*) — customary greeting when approaching a neighbour's home

Karibu (*kah-**ree**-boo*) — you're welcome

Mama (***ma**-ma*) — title of honour for a woman

Mzee (*mm-**zay***) — title of honour for a man

Rafiki (*rah-**fee**-key*) — friend

Facts About Kenya

You can fit France inside Kenya with a little room to spare.

To walk across Kenya, from Lake Victoria to the Indian Ocean, would take over one million steps.

The Great Rift Valley, one of the most spectacular geological features on earth, runs through Kenya. It is a geological fault that will eventually break East Africa off to form an island.

Mount Kenya is the second highest spot in Africa. Even though it's on the equator, it's covered with snow.

Lake Victoria, on Kenya's western border, is the third largest lake in the world. It is part of the White Nile. The largest lake in Kenya is Lake Turkana, in the north.

Nairobi is Kenya's capital city. Maasai cattle herders who used this land called it 'enkare nyarobe', which means 'cool water country'.

The main seaport of Mombasa was settled by Arab traders over a thousand years ago. It is an important link between Kenya and the rest of the world.

Wildlife parks in Kenya have protected borders where some endangered animal species live. Tsavo National Park is the largest reserve, and the Maasai Mara is one of the most popular with tourists.

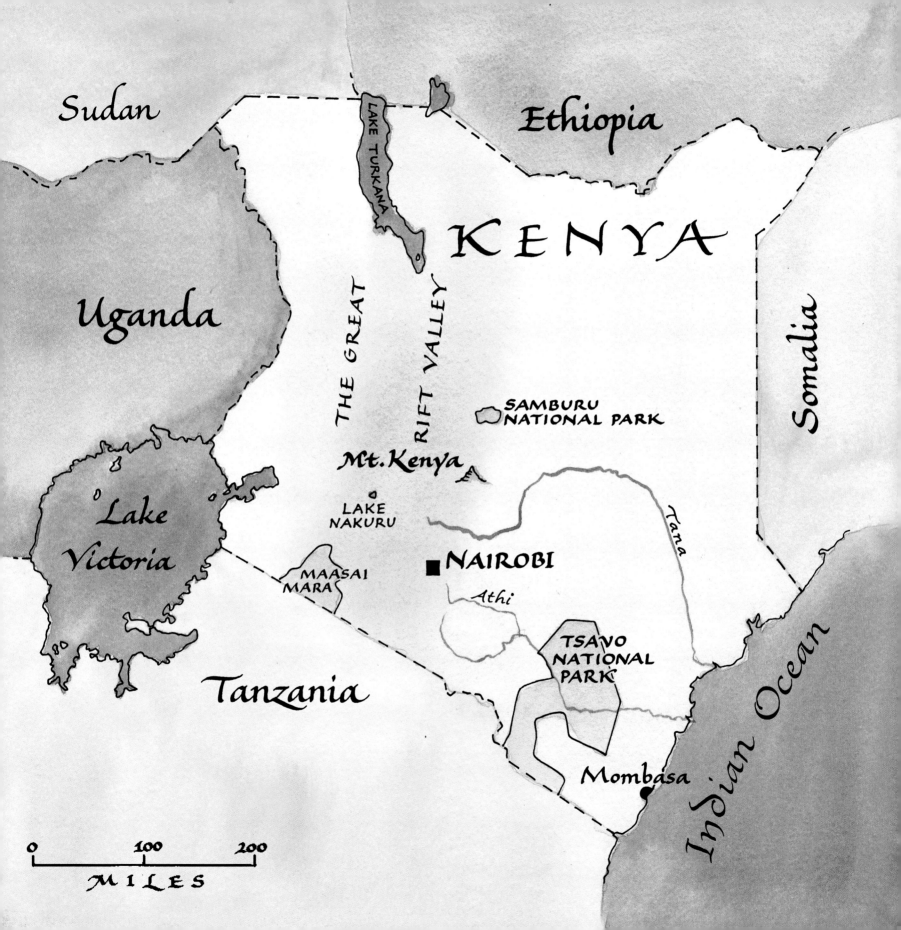

Sudan

Ethiopia

LAKE TURKANA

KENYA

Uganda

THE GREAT

RIFT VALLEY

Somalia

SAMBURU
NATIONAL PARK

Mt. Kenya

Lake
Victoria

LAKE
NAKURU

Tana

NAIROBI

Athi

MAASAI
MARA

TSAVO
NATIONAL
PARK

Tanzania

Indian Ocean

Mombasa

0   100   200
M I L E S

Mama Panya's Pancakes

Pancakes are eaten all around the world. They have different names in different countries. Here are a few examples: Scotland — bannocks, India — chapati, France — crêpes, China — bao bing, Russia — blinis, Indonesia — dadar gutung, Egypt — qata'if, Chile — arepas, Mexico — tortillas.

Many Kenyans like to wrap food inside thin pancakes. Would you like to try Mama Panya's pancakes? Here's a recipe that you can make at home:

Ingredients (makes about six pancakes)
115-170gms plain flour
500ml cold water
5 tablespoons sunflower oil
$\frac{1}{2}$ teaspoon salt
$\frac{1}{2}$ teaspoon cardamom (or nutmeg will do)
$\frac{1}{2}$ teaspoon red chilli pepper flakes, crushed

Instructions
In a bowl, mix all the ingredients with a fork.
Pre-heat a non-stick pan (no oil is needed) at a medium to low setting.
Ladle $\frac{1}{4}$ cup of batter into the centre of the pan. Tilt the pan to spread the batter to about the size of a grapefruit.
Cook until you see tiny bubbles in the pancake, then gently flip it over.
When the second side begins to pop up from the heat, the pancake is ready.

Serving Suggestions
You can fill your pancake with jam for something sweet, or tuna salad for something savoury. In fact, almost any filling will do. Simply roll up and eat!

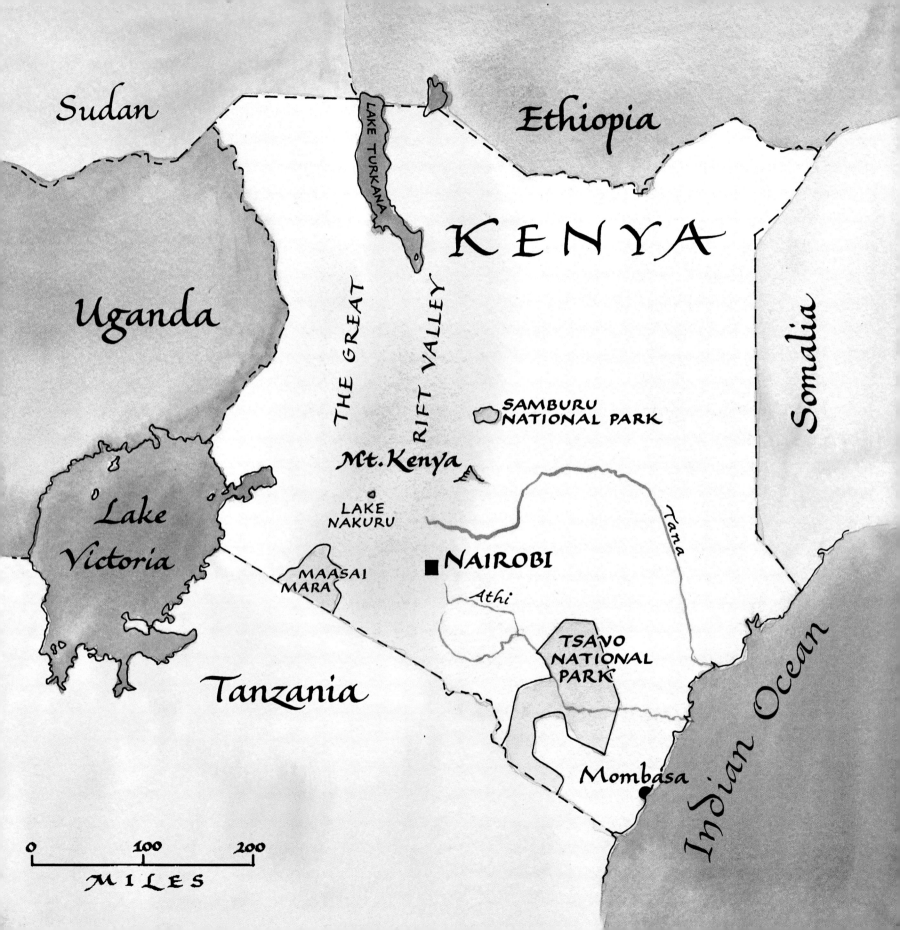

Mama Panya's Pancakes

Pancakes are eaten all around the world. They have different names in different countries. Here are a few examples: Scotland — bannocks, India — chapati, France — crêpes, China — bao bing, Russia — blinis, Indonesia — dadar gutung, Egypt — qata'if, Chile — arepas, Mexico — tortillas.

Many Kenyans like to wrap food inside thin pancakes. Would you like to try Mama Panya's pancakes? Here's a recipe that you can make at home:

Ingredients (makes about six pancakes)
115-170gms plain flour
500ml cold water
5 tablespoons sunflower oil
$^1/_2$ teaspoon salt
$^1/_2$ teaspoon cardamom (or nutmeg will do)
$^1/_2$ teaspoon red chilli pepper flakes, crushed

Instructions
In a bowl, mix all the ingredients with a fork.
Pre-heat a non-stick pan (no oil is needed) at a medium to low setting.
Ladle $^1/_4$ cup of batter into the centre of the pan. Tilt the pan to spread the batter to about the size of a grapefruit.
Cook until you see tiny bubbles in the pancake, then gently flip it over.
When the second side begins to pop up from the heat, the pancake is ready.

Serving Suggestions
You can fill your pancake with jam for something sweet, or tuna salad for something savoury. In fact, almost any filling will do. Simply roll up and eat!

Barefoot Books
Celebrating Art and Story

At Barefoot Books, we celebrate art and story with books that open
the hearts and minds of children from all walks of life, inspiring them to read
deeper, search further, and explore their own creative gifts. Taking our
inspiration from many different cultures, we focus on themes that encourage
independence of spirit, enthusiasm for learning, and acceptance of other
traditions. Thoughtfully prepared by writers, artists and storytellers from
all over the world, our products combine the best of the present with the best
of the past to educate our children as the caretakers of tomorrow.

www.barefootbooks.com